PARABLES

seema agarwal

PARABLES

BALBOA.
PRESS

A DIVISION OF HAY HOUSE

Balboa Press books may be ordered through booksellers or by contacting:

Balboa Press
A Division of Hay House
1663 Liberty Drive
Bloomington, IN 47403
www.balboapress.com
1-(877) 407-4847

Because of the dynamic nature of the Internet, any web addresses or
links contained in this book may have changed since publication and
may no longer be valid. The views expressed in this work are solely those
of the author and do not necessarily reflect the views of the publisher,
and the publisher hereby disclaims any responsibility for them.

The author of this book does not dispense medical advice or prescribe the use
of any technique as a form of treatment for physical, emotional, or medical
problems without the advice of a physician, either directly or indirectly. The
intent of the author is only to offer information of a general nature to help
you in your quest for emotional and spiritual well-being. In the event you use
any of the information in this book for yourself, which is your constitutional
right, the author and the publisher assume no responsibility for your actions.

Certain stock imagery © Thinkstock.
Any people depicted in stock imagery provided by Thinkstock are
models, and such images are being used for illustrative purposes only.

ISBN: 978-1-4525-3934-8 (e)
ISBN: 978-1-4525-3935-5 (sc)

Printed in the United States of America

Balboa Press rev. date: 9/14/2011

Foreword

Learning from every thing and being costitutes the spiritual practice. The nine stories in this book of Seema is her creative attempt to initiate the readers to this art of learning. When we learn from every experience of our lives we grow wise and do not create dents and wounds on our mind like likes and dislikes. This process of purification of mind is aimed at in this wonderful book of parables. Seema has grown in her spiritual unfoldment through this process by learning from the various events of her life and this book is the result of this learning. Stop aging by constant learning!!!

–Swami Anubhavananda

Acknowledgement

The presence Who is always with me even when i am absent, first and foremost, i would like to thank Him. He gives me hope, strength and faith to carry on with myself. He is the One who is there when no one else is. He is the One who supports, guides and lights the way of my life.

Anil, my husband and best friend, has been a loving guide through thick and thin! I am deeply grateful for his grounding presence in my life. My kids, Aniruddh and Devvrat, who do drive me nuts at times but are also the reason for my still being sane; My parents, Dr. Ved Prakash and Aruna Bindal for ingraining in me the essence, that is the glue that holds me together; My brother, sisters, friends, relatives, elders, kids and my whole universal family, who are all an essential part of me, Thank you all.....

Swami Anubhavananda, whose faith in me, reawakened my faith in myself; Mr. Nair, my role model, for all the selfless work that he does;

I cannot miss thanking the people who went through my work and gave me their vital opinions, suggestions and comments.

I sincerely thank you, the reader and the seeker. You have spent your precious time, money and energy in buying this book! Thank you from the bottom of my heart! I hope to do justice to your expectations.

Dedication

this book is dedicated
to
'you'
the reader.......
the seeker.......

The way of love is not
A subtle argument.
The door there is devastation.
Birds make great sky-circles of their freedom.
How do they learn it?
They fall, and falling,
They're given wings.

-Rumi

Aglio the Eaglet

I was whirling through the air at breakneck speed! I couldn't stop! I could hear Mom crying out for me and I was screaming at the top of my lungs, too! Lower and lower I fell into a vortex and I was sure that I was about to die...........

Mom had gotten us to the edge of the cliff. She was going to teach us to fly. I had seen her flying often enough and though it seemed exciting to my brothers and sister, I was terrified of it, even then. Doubts had assailed me, 'What if I cannot fly?' 'Will my Mom still love me, if I fail, or will she tear me apart like my friends' Mom had done, and throw me off the cliff?' The suspense was too much to bear but it had been better than when the day finally dawned.

We were taken on Mom's back to the cliff edge. She took us one by one on her back and left us when we were sufficiently airborne. She had guided us through the process till we learnt how to fly. 'I will be there, Aglio, you have nothing to fear. Trust me and trust this process. We all do this. It is a part of who we are. It is exhilarating, really....you will love it once you learn. You will hardly want to set foot on ground again', she had said before taking me up in the air. She knew I was terrified. After all, I had been a witness to what had happened to my dear friend, Angelo. I could still hear his screams in my ears.

Mom had finished with Agolo, Egel and Angela. They had all come out flying. They looked ecstatic! Their success made me feel somehow worse. 'What if I couldn't do it?' And then all too soon, it was my turn. I was shivering with fear but I tried not to show it. I got on to Mom's back. She could sense my fear but she soothingly told me to have faith.

As we went soaring into the air, I gripped her back as though my life depended on it, and it did. All of a sudden, she jerked me free and went down with such speed that I could not clutch her anymore. I was left on my own. I was so scared that I couldn't think straight. I forgot all the instructions she had given me. I couldn't be calm and relaxed as she had told me to be. I couldn't listen to my instincts which would be my teacher from this moment on. I was so weak because of the fear that I was afraid I was losing consciousness. With half open eyes I saw my Mom trying to reach me. She was getting closer and just when I thought I would be saved, she was attacked by another larger bird. The three of us got tangled but then before I knew what was happening, I was falling again. Falling with such speed and all I could see was my Mom. Her eyes. The helplessness and frustration in them....she knew after all that she was the only person in the world I had trusted.

As I fell through the abyss, I thought that there was no hope for me now. I heard somebody say, 'Aglio, you can do this.' 'Who is this?' 'That does not matter, just be calm and spread your wings.' I closed my eyes. I thought of my Mom and the love we had shared. I must try, if only for her sake….. the fear was greatly diminished as I was ready to face death if need be. And then, just a few feet from the ground, I gave up all resistance and opened up my wings. It was as if, that was all that had been needed from my side. I was buoyed up into the air. I was being supported by the very air that had seemed my enemy a few seconds before. I was flying, by jove, and it was fantastic. I just cannot describe it in words! It was the best experience of my life. I was so overjoyed…. and just then the reality came down crashing on me. How would I face Mom again? My brothers and sister must be laughing at my failure! I couldn't go back. I had failed them. I had nearly killed myself and I knew that was really shameful for those of my kind. It was now or never with them. After all, Angelo had not been given another chance. Why would they accept me again? My failure had been worse than my success now and it would have been better had I crashed and died, there on that very floor visible to my now blurred eyes. 'Oh Mom, I am so sorry……I let you down…….'

In the next couple of days, I tried and tested my wings in all ways possible. There was nothing else for me to do. Nobody to talk to. Nobody to play with. So, I entertained myself with silly tricks. There would be times when I would feel low. Kind of depressed. It was mostly when I missed my Mom. She had been my support system for so many days. She had understood everything about me, my needs and wants, my fears and insecurities, what made me happy and what didn't. She loved me and I loved her. But now, the wall of failure stood between us. I knew I could go back. What kept me from doing that was the disappointment I would have to face. That would be too much to bear. I could remain dead for her, but my life now meant that I couldn't go back. Self respect was the world to us eagles. I would not want to lower my Mom in her own eyes because of me.

'Aglio, give her a chance. Trust her', said my invisible companion on one such day, that I was depressed. As he said these words, I broke down. In that instant, it came crashing down on me, that I had been blaming her, too, for my predicament. I was not the only one to blame, was I. I had trusted her. She had said she would be there, no matter what. Not only had I failed, but she had failed too. She had let me go down to die, in front of her eyes.

I had waited......waited for her to come swooping down for me......waited till the near end was in sight. I had believed that she would be there. She wouldn't just leave me to die .....and then, all my expectations had come crashing down like a ton of bricks. She had let me go. She had let me fall to my near death. No. I could not go back. It was then that it dawned on me, I was not scared of reading disappointment in her eyes. I was afraid that my disappointment would show in my eyes. I was not sure if I could ever be the same again.

If there was one thing that I enjoyed, it was flying. I zoomed about up and down. I did wheelies in the air and grew stronger and bolder every day. One evening there was a storm brewing. Now, instead of being afraid, I flew straight into the eye of the storm and did some of my best flying! I was on top of the world. 'If only my family could see me now,' I pondered wistfully.

'Go home, Aglio', my friend suggested. 'Give them a chance. Give yourself a chance.' I still wasn't sure. That night I fretted and fumed in my dreams. I saw that the big bird had caught my Mom and was eating her alive!' I screamed in my sleep and woke up feeling the same helplessness I had seen in my Mom's eyes. As I slowly got into the air, I saw the sun coming up in beautiful shades of reddish orange, up the horizon. 'Go home… Aglio…. Go home…..'

Tears blurred my vision now but I knew I must do this. I would go home. I would just have a quick look to see if she was safe and come back. I wouldn't let her see me. As I took off, hope and despair both filled my heart. What if she was dead? Would I be able to take that? Was that why she had not come after me? But, then hope would fill my heart, 'No, nothing could have happened to her…..'

I was nearly by the edge of the cliff. I would be by our nest in no time now. I slowed down……..everything seemed to be happening in slow motion. I neared the nest. There she was! I could see my Mom. Her head was bent low and she seemed to be deep in thought about something. As I drew nearer, I saw that she had a far off expression in her eyes and looked dejected and lost. I had meant to take one look at her and go, but my feet and wings seemed to have no strength left. Her expression was so haunted that I just couldn't bring myself to go. I just sat there, a few feet away from her. She looked up as soon as she felt my presence. I could see relief and happiness painted all over her face. 'Aglio…….It is you, isn't it…….I knew you would come'. Before I could say a word, she fell off the branch and landed with a loud thud on the ground. I rushed to her side and shook her vehemently. 'Mom…….Yes, it is me……wake up Ma..I'm so sorry…I let u down Ma….'. As I was wondering what to do next, looking about frantically, she opened her eyes. 'Aglio, my dearest child…….No…you were great…. you were so brave. The bravest of the lot, I must say......and I was certain you would come. I have not left this perch since that day, dear, for I knew with conviction, that you would come back...you have no need to be sorry....you did not let me down, it was me who did that to you.....please forgive me dear, for I love you dearly.......'

'Bbut, why didn't you....how could you......?' I couldn't bring myself to ask the question that had been haunting me day and night. I couldn't ask her why she had not come for me. But as usual, I did not have to even voice the whole sentence. Mom understood. 'I couldn't, dear, I couldn't. If I had come, like my heart told me to, you would not have been able to live with the fact that you had not been able to fly. You would not have lived through that even if I would give you a second chance, going against all protocol. You would not have given yourself a second chance. The moment you dropped out of my sight, I fought off that other bird, I knew that I should come for you..... but then something stopped me. My instincts told me that the journey back would have to be made by you, and you alone. Help meant death. Whether physical death or mental death. In any case you would have died. I braced myself with immense courage, which came from a part within, and let you go. I have never felt worse in my life, than at that moment, Aglio. But, my instincts also told me that you would come. Every moment I have only been praying for your well-being, protection, guidance and return. I am so happy that you found your way home. You faced your fears, your hurt, disappointments, and you came back. Welcome into the real world, son. This world is an eagle eat eagle world. You have to be strong to rule the roost, here. After all, how long will I be able to protect and guide you. You have after all, learnt not only flying, but you have the best guide you will ever have, forever more. Your own instincts have found a way of reaching out to you. You found a way of listening to them. What more could a mother want for her dear children? What more could I want for you, Aglio?'

While we had been talking, Egel, Angelo and Agolo had appeared. We neck hugged each other with teary eyes. 'Mom just hasn't been the same without you. She wouldn't eat or drink. She has only been waiting for you, Aglio. We all missed you, bro, don't ever scare the life out of us, ever again, get that!' Angela threatened. As we got talking, I showed them the neat tricks I had learnt by myself. They were so impressed. They showed me their flying and we laughed, played and flew together. All of us repented the time lost, but also looked forward to the brighter tomorrow.

When I got a moment alone, I thanked my invisible friend silently. I was so full of gratitude that I could barely express it in words. I could not believe that I had decided not to come back. How could I have even thought of a life without my loved ones? I had been postponing coming back for so many days. I had outdone myself with my fantasies. I knew now in my heart of hearts, that I had never failed my mother, nor had she ever failed me. This was merely something I had to learn for myself. My mother would never have torn me apart, like Angelo's mom had done. She would have died before she had to do that. In my heart, I also knew that I had not trusted her enough; had not trusted the process enough; and had not trusted myself enough. But, all that had also taught me an important lesson. Facing fears, gathering courage, braving a storm could only be possible if two main ingredients were there; love and faith.

When it happened I had no clue. When I had surrendered I did not know. But, without knowing it, I had learnt the biggest lesson of my whole life, which would now make living a veritable joy. I had learnt to let go. I had been ready to face death and a joyless existence. I had come back home after a long journey in the wilderness. I had now learnt to trust myself, the process and others. I now knew that love never dies....... it only grows....... I was ready to take on the world......... I was home......

Trying to be perfect may be inevitable for people who are smart and ambitious; who are interested in the world and its good opinion .... what is really hard, and really amazing, is giving up on being perfect and beginning the work of becoming yourself.

-Anna Quindlen

Bilva the Bulb

The temple of Sri Krishna in the midst of the deep forest was frequently visited by the neighboring villagers. Some of them would come in the morning and stay till evening; it was so peaceful. The temple was a small one; the pujari stayed in the back with his family.

Bilva was the bulb that illuminated the glory of Sri Krishna. It was a magnificent sight and visitors were held in awe just looking at the idol. It was dressed in the richest of fabrics, adorned by the most magnificent jewels. It was truly a wondrous sight which left the devotees spellbound.

Whenever devotees stood in humility and gratitude, Bilva's ego bloated no end. He was very proud to be the one illuminating this glorious vision; in fact, his pride bordered on arrogance. He would constantly ridicule the other bulbs in the room. 'I have the most important job in this temple. Look at you all…….Ha Ha………it is a joke! You are merely illuminating ordinary things and beings. And Koli has the most demeaning of all jobs! He has to illuminate the toilet! Of all the places! I would certainly die if that was my fate. Thank God I am here, where I am!'

The other bulbs did not like being ridiculed and they did not like the way he put down Koli. He was a nice guy after all; it was not his fault that he had the job of illuminating the toilet. But, they also knew that they could never win an argument with Bilva. He was so pompous, loud and boisterous. Anything they said fell on deaf ears. And they would only wind up feeling worse.

Their lives happily went by, lighting up the place and feeling good just being a part of the temple. When they were not on duty, they would meet within the wires and have a blast. They had one thing that Bilva did not; they had each other. They were all thick buddies, even with Koli, who was an extremely fun loving guy. He had no hang-ups about his job. He did not feel it was demeaning in any way. It was just a thing to be done and he did just that.

Bilva used to be jealous of their camaraderie but then he reminded himself, he had God. What else was there that was more important? Not a single thing. He would not trade his place for anything in the world. He was so content with his place in life. His life began and ended with his illuminating the idol. When he was not on duty, he would think about his luck and pat himself on the back. 'I must have done something really good to be this fortunate. This is all like a dream come true. I really have it made. Not like those losers. They must be getting punishment for the bad things they have done in life.'

For Bilva it was all a one man show. It was always about him and his good fortune. It went on to such an extent that his bragging started getting on all the bulbs' filaments. They could tolerate him no more! They wished sincerely that he just shut up and stop the intolerable act of blowing his own trumpet.

It seemed like their wish was about to come true. On one opportune evening, after the *aarti,* it so happened, that Koli went out. It was so sudden. One moment he was hale and hearty and the next, he was gone. The news came as a sad shock amongst all the light bulbs. The only one who had a good laugh was Bilva. 'Thank God, that unlucky wretch is gone!' Little was Bilva to know what lay in store for him.

'Let us put that new colorful bulb we got to illuminate the idol' said the Pujari. The sevak quickly ran and got the box of new bulbs. They were all of different colors. The sevak said, 'Why don't we put a new color every day? It will look very attractive and make our temple more popular.'

The pujari agreed and they did just that. The sevak removed Bilva and put him down. He then put one of the red colored bulbs in the holder. They could not see or hear Bilva, and that was good, because Bilva was screaming in agony. He was deeply hurt, angry and frustrated. He was lashing out in pain. He wanted to go back to his home; but they had ruthlessly snatched away his home from him.

'Oh Krishna, are you seeing how they are taking me away from you? I want to stay here, next to you. Please do something. Help me. I will die if I am kept away from you, Krishna'.

Bilva was being taken away and to his utter dismay and horror, he saw that he was being taken to the toilet. 'This is a nightmare. It is worse than a nightmare. This cannot be happening to me! To Bilva! It just cannot! I was the chosen one......the favorite.

How can this be so? I do not want to go there. I do not want to take Koli's place. I would rather die, God. Please come to my aid!'

And thus began Bilva's truly humbling journey; his journey home. Not next to the idol of God but next to God himself. Though it was not easy; but then who says life is easy? Though Bilva often felt life was unfair; but then who says life is fair? Bilva often felt like the road was all uphill but then who says you are going to have a smooth journey? Bilva often felt as though he was all alone; at those very times he discovered he was not. After a long strenuous unending struggle, he felt what true joy was.

The beginning was the toughest. Bilva withdrew into his filaments. He did not want to talk to anybody. In fact, he wanted to die. He literally tried all he could to fuse his light. He could not succeed. He had thought he was in control till he discovered that he had no control whatsoever. His life and death were not in his filaments. He could not choose when to light up, when to not. He could not choose where he wanted to be. He was only a bulb in the hands of others who controlled it. The first thing that started changing and mellowing Bilva, was when his bloated ego started leaving him.

His duty was now only in the toilet, the very place he had hated with all his heart. 'What did I do to deserve this?' He would keep questioning God, though no answers gave him respite.

Then one day when his guard was down, a new bulb that had just come into the temple, made her way towards Bilva and greeted him, when they were both off-duty. 'Hi Bilva, I am

Sunahiri. I am new here. Will you show me around?' Bilva tried to ignore her but she was bent on becoming his friend. The other bulbs warned her about him, but Sunahiri found him irresistible. She would come to him whenever she was free.

Bilva resisted her at first but soon was bowled over by her persistence. He wondered why she was attracted to him, when all others were repelled. He started moving around with her when they were both off-duty. They chatted and laughed; they shared their deepest secrets; they became the closest of buddies in the temple.

Bilva had earlier thought that he had all the answers. That he knew everything there was to be known. Boy, had he been wrong! After meeting Sunahiri, Bilva realized just how ignorant he had been; so full of himself; so obnoxious.

Sunahiri taught him that they were all a part of one big whole. That whole, whose name was electricity, was a universal energy. Bulbs were just a manifestation of that whole, and could not function all by themselves. She told him about the interconnectedness between the energy, electricity, the wires and the bulbs. She explained how many bulbs thought they were in control because they could be seen and felt and could not digest the fact that actually it was energy that was in control, because energy could not be seen or touched.

'Bilva, when you were illuminating the idol, you were not more special than any other bulb. Now that you are in the toilet, it does not mean that it is a punishment of any sort. When you were in front of the idol, you were required to do your duty. Now that you are in the toilet, you are still required to do only your duty. The duty is not assigned by you. The duty is assigned by the energy that drives each one of us. That too, only till the time that we are capable of discharging our duties. Koli's time was up. He had done his duties well and lived his life to the full. For him, it was not a demeaning job for he knew that he was a mere instrument in this game of light. It did not feed his ego nor did it subtract even a little from his self-esteem to do whatever jobs came his way. He showed all of us the true meaning of living and loving. Though he had the worst duty, he was always happy and friendly to all. Though you had the seemingly most sought for duty, still you were always alone. The duty is not what makes us who we are, Bilva, it is we who make our duty what it is.'

Bilva was embarrassed by the way he had been behaving with the others. He was feeling terrible because of the pompous fool he had been. There had been innumerable times when the other bulbs wanted to befriend him. But, he had thought it to be below his status to mingle with them. He wished he could take that all back and be friends with them.

Here again, Sunahiri came to the rescue. It truly seemed like she was a god-send. She got him to meet Lolu, Sura, Wali and Gunjan. They forgave Bilva so easily that he had tears in his filaments. He was so fortunate to have such precious friends. They showed him how they all could meet in one place and then have a blast together. Bilva started living, truly living, for the very first time in his life. He felt loved, which was the most amazing feeling. Better even than illuminating the idol of Sri Krishna. Love flowed through all the wires and made his filaments tingle with the glorious feeling of being alive.

It was a humbling moment for Bilva, when once again he was removed from his holder. The best part was that the helplessness, frustration and struggle were gone. The fear and worry was gone. He now knew that wherever he went, he would do his job the best he could.

'These colored lights are useless! They don't show the idol in its true glory!', said the Pujari to the sevak. 'Change the bulb again. Replace it with this one that was there before. This is the brightest one we have. Put that new bulb we got a few days ago in the toilet.'

As Bilva shone in his glory one more time, illuminating Sri Krishna, he sent thanks to Sunahiri who had now taken his place in his old home, the toilet!

Courage is the price that life exacts for granting peace.
- Amelia Earhart

Grace and Her Course

"**H**ow can I disappear into obscurity? What will happen of me, Grace, if I go the course meant for me? How can I be willing to allow each particle of 'me' to go separate ways? Who knows into how many million bits will I be divided and destroyed? Am I ready for this? Am I willing to die? Give up my name and identity? And for what? Why? What do I gain? I only see myself losing........ in every which way. How can I surrender myself to a hole so deep and black, from where no hope and light seems to be visible. Maybe that fate is inevitable and I can stall for only so long........but for now, I'm not ready."

Grace the River, meandered on a pathway for the nth time. This was not the first time she had struggled with herself on this matter. She had meandered on unknown pathways umpteen number of times. She couldn't bring herself to merge with the ocean as easily as so many of her sisters and relatives. She came this close........then turned away before it was too late.

Grace was a beautiful and bubbly river with crystal clear, blue, pure water. Her sisters had always been envious of her since her birth. Her beauty was ethereal. It was just so different and unique. She was not even aware of this difference and beauty. She was just engrossed in each moment. How each part of her altered and changed. How she lost some parts of herself on river banks, added some parts when it rained. It was such an awesome feeling. Never did it cross Grace's mind that the rain water merged with her with no qualms of non-existence. But, when she lost parts of herself, she mourned them for awhile. There was nothing really she could do, and she resigned herself to this fate. Every day was a new experience for her. Visiting new places; meeting different people; hugging unique contours of this rich earth. She loved her life! She would not exchange this for anything.

She went about her life with a spring in each wave; A bounce on every turn. Hers was an inspired life and she brought about positivity in the air every which way she went. The mountains, the earth, the air and the sun, all basked in her glory. Such an effect had she on others. As she made them smile and sing, so in turn did they. This was the beautiful way in which she expressed her gratitude to the world by honoring herself.

It soon became so, that each part of her rejoiced when she decided to meander once more. Stall some more and avoid one more time, her inevitable fate. What if she lost her charm once she became one with the vast ocean? The universal vastness of the ocean would wash off her smile and bounce, she feared.

This process would have gone on and on. It could have become an endless undertaking had Grace not witnessed for herself and seen what became of others who opted for obscurity. She had been a witness since her birth actually, but she had not been able to accept it. She saw but behaved like she couldn't. She understood but was not ready to try it for herself. It was happening every minute of every day. But for Grace the time had not yet come.

As they say, when the student is ready, the teacher appears. Grace knew, saw, understood but acceptance was what she lacked. One day the earth vibrated with new life. Her long time friend Nimi, the Neem seed, had cracked open. She was gone and in her place, from her heart could be seen a stem coming up and roots going below. Oh Nimi, where have you gone….. Grace was upset at the death of her friend. They had been growing close by the day. Why had Nimi not stalled, the way she had been stalling? She would have lived longer………

As Grace mourned for Nimi, she thought she was hallucinating. She could hear Nimi's voice and it was singing! "I am not nothing. I am everything. I am not dead, Grace…..I am alive!" Grace was astounded! "Where are you, I cannot see you, Nimi?" "I am right here, where I used to be. Grace, I cannot explain this feeling of fulfillment that I am feeling. You know when I was going to crack open, I felt like I was dying a million deaths. I found myself thinking 'I am nothing', and then I cracked open. I feared my existence would come to an end. I was ready to merge into nothingness. Then it happened, Grace. I was not nothing, I was everything. I did not die, I was born. On the very brink of destruction, I found myself. Yes, I have changed externally and internally. Externally you can very well see. Internally I can only hope that you understand. I have expanded and grown like I could never have imagined. What a meek existence was I before this. I thought I would die. I thought my end was near. Boy, was I ever wrong! Grace, I was not created or destroyed, I merely got transformed from one form to another!"

Grace was confused. Of course, she saw it happening day in and day out. Seeds bursting into plants and trees, leaves falling, stones breaking, rivers merging, eggs cracking, caterpillars transforming, butterflies emerging, water evaporating and condensing. She knew this was all the cycle of life. This happened to everyone else and would one day happen to her. She would cross that bridge when she came to it, Grace thought once again.

She lost friends in her journey as they traveled on, moving to greener pastures. She made new friends too. She lost parts of herself and she gained some, too. Some parts of herself were no longer averse to joining the ocean. They were the ones who at some point had left her and rejoined her at a later stage. They would tell her, we all are connected Grace. The ocean is not our enemy. It does not wish to take our identity away from us. In fact, it wants to show us how much bigger and better we can be. We will not die or fade away into obscurity, Grace, if anything, we will expand and only grow. Their well-meaning words would generally fall on deaf ears. Grace was not ready yet. She meandered here and there and everywhere. She only kept away from the ocean. Her struggle for maintaining her own identity, seemed to take its toll on her.

She was rapidly losing her good cheer and charm. She was contracting as many of her parts were leaving her and going away. It seemed like she forgot that she could smile, sing or dance again. Her bounce was lost. The spring in her waves was gone and it seemed like she brought about her own non-existence like a self-fulfilling prophecy by being so worried and tense about it all the time.

The earth, sky, wind and sun all noticed her dying before their very eyes. They tried talking to her. Grace, look at yourself!

What are you doing? Please see that you, because of your fears, are destroying yourself. Grace found everyone to be her enemy, now. She would brush them off, 'better to be destroyed like this, don't you think, rather than merging into an endless abyss?'

The day was close. She had shrunk like never before. She was getting to be a mere trickle and if she did not change her mind, yet, she would certainly die a meaningless death.

The sun shone down brightly on her, more parts of herself leaving her and joining the expanse of nothingness. It was now or never. The brink of her destruction. Was she ready? 'Grace, you can do it!', cried out her friend Cloud. "Grace, we are with you, you can do it!", cried out the earth below her belly. One by one, Grace heard friends from near and far, asking her to join the ocean. But, what really made her change her mind was the loving voice which came to her after all were quiet. "Grace, I have waited for you since eternity. Will you not give me the honor of your presence? I am not your enemy, Grace, I am your friend. I am nothing else, but a part of you and you are nothing else but a part of me. We are not two, Grace, we are one......"

On hearing the voice of the ocean, Grace was transported back to eons ago, when in fact, the ocean, Grace, and all the waters upon the earth, had been one. She now knew how they all were interconnected. Not just the waters, but the earth, sky, sun, wind, people, seeds, plants, trees, animals, insects, everything that was Created by the Universal Creator, was so very intertwined and intermingled. How could one think of oneself as a separate existence and entity as she had?

"Yes! Yes! I wish to join you Ocean! In fact, whether I physically am able to join you or not, I don't know. It may be that I have taken this decision too late. But, I do know that I will not die even if all parts of me, leave me and go. They are already interconnected. I will only be transformed for awhile. But, eventually, I will join you!"

It seemed like Grace had only to say 'Yes.' Cloud burst and let many parts of Grace join her again. The earth seemed to carry her with a force that Grace had never witnessed. The wind moved her with a speed unmatched and unrivalled. The sun shone a lot less brightly and tried to disappear behind Cloud, lest some parts of Grace leave her again. The sky became her guide and showed her the way towards Ocean.

Just a few moments ago, on the brink of her destruction, Grace had found the will to live again. Live a free life. A life free of fear, worry and tension. A life which could be with or without identity. A life which may or may not have meaning. But, importantly, Grace had given Life one more chance.

Grace reached Ocean. She merged every part of herself wholeheartedly with every part of the ocean. She vibrated with a new found freedom. She was not nothing. She was everything. She was not dead, she was as alive as she had ever been. She did not fade into obscurity, rather, the ocean bounced with a new vitality, a fresh energy as nothing and everything merged into one!

We all have our own life to pursue, our own kind of dream to be weaving. And we all have some power to make wishes come true; as long as we keep believing.

- Louisa May Alcott

Kachchua the Slow-poke

It was that time of the year again. The Annual Race-off was round the corner. All the animals in Jungli Land were preparing for it. The last few days had been very exciting for most of the animals and they were looking forward to the Race-off.

Kachchua, unfortunately, was not one among those. He was dreading this event even though he had secretly been preparing himself since the whole of last year. He had always been the one who came last in every year's race and hence had been named Slow-poke. Everyone poked fun at him for being the slowest animal around! It was so embarrassing and Kachchua would do anything to change this. Year after year he had been the brunt of many jokes and ridicule. At first he would laugh at himself. Then he did not find it funny anymore but the animals were too used to him being the brunt of all their jokes and he could do nothing to change that.

Kachchua had been such a meek turtle always; since as far as he could remember. So, when these horrible thoughts and feelings started attacking him, he did not know what to do. It had started a couple of years ago, after he came in last once again. As usual there had been a huge celebration for Cheetah, who always came first, and just as huge a celebration for Kachchua as he had come in last for the umpteenth time. Kachchua had not been his normal self that day. He couldn't just shake off their bantering and teasing. That night, he literally went into his shell for several days.

He had never felt so helpless ever before. He was feeling the victim, where on his expense others used to get great joy and entertainment. He had not minded that earlier and had taken it in his stride (however slow that might be). But, something snapped in him that night. He was feeling a burning from within. He wanted to lash out at somebody or something. He was boiling from inside but he did not know what to do about it. He was feeling absolutely horrible about himself and what was even worse, was that he started feeling horribly about everyone around him. It seemed like he compared his body to theirs and he always fell short. They had one thing or the other that was better that what he had. Cheetah, especially was the very bane of his existence. Not only was he the fastest amongst them, but he had such a great body. You could spend hours just admiring him. He was so sleek and good-looking. All the girls were crazy about him!

But, the other animals too had it made. Whether he observed the fox, wolf, lion, elephant, dog, deer, cat or even the rabbit, he felt they all were better than him. He began to elevate others to a pedestal and cut himself short every chance he got. He put himself down to such an extent that he started feeling a different kind of burning from within. This burning was the kind which made him feel worse when he saw the success of any other animal. It only exaggerated and accentuated his failure. This burning was intolerable. It was even worse than the burning which came up once in a while, because that burning went away after some time. He would cool off by slipping into the water, seeing the awesome sun setting or moon rising. When he would sit with nature and witness its magnificence, his feelings of unworthiness and rage at others would melt away.

But, this other burning became a part of his skin. It became a part of his body, mind and soul. He would not shake with anger when he felt like this, nor cry in helplessness. This burning became a part of his nature so quickly and smoothly that he was hardly aware when it took over him. It slowly started eating him up from inside. The feeling was: jealousy. It happened when he would compare himself to others which was occasional in the beginning. He would feel they are better and he is not good enough. Then this feeling soon became a vital part of Kachchua because it seemed like he was constantly comparing himself to others and he was the one who had the shorter end of the stick.

Now, it was no longer just the race, he let it spread like a virus, to every area of his life. He was out to prove what to whom he did not know. But, he knew that he did have to prove something. If not to anybody else, to himself surely, the need was apparent.

The morning of the race dawned bright and sunny. The starting line had Cheetah, Wolf, Cat, Dog, Deer, Rabbit, Elk, Antelope, Pig, Mouse, Elephant, Kachchua and Bear. Sloth, who had stopped taking part in the race eons ago, had been given the responsibility of Manager for the race. He hit the start clap and the race was on.

Kachchua had been preparing all year. This was one year he was determined not to come in last. He started well and gave it his best shot. Cheetah, of course was nowhere in sight. But, Kachchua was observing whom he could defeat rather than see where Cheetah had reached. He noticed that Mouse was awfully slow this year. He could stop and ask him what was wrong, but Kachchua saw this as the opportunity he had been waiting for. He raced ahead of Mouse and tried to keep his speed as high as he could. He was not far behind Pig. He knew he could do it. He could beat Pig too. His reserve of energy was coming in handy and Kachchua seemed to be getting ahead of Pig. He was overjoyed and ecstatic. Now, he just had to maintain this speed. He could do it, of that he was sure. Soon he left Pig behind as he raced on. He would show them this year that he was not the slowest of them all.

As Kachchua went by the rose bush at the turning of the last lap, he saw that Cat was lying unconscious. He lay a few feet ahead of him. No help seemed to be in sight. Jackal was in charge of cases like these. He made rounds and saw to it if anyone needed his help. Jackal was nowhere to be seen. Kachchua did not have a second to waste. He knew that helping Cat meant running the risk of coming in last once again. He would just have to leave Cat and hope that Jackal would find him soon. But, as he neared Cat, he saw that his breathing was very erratic. He was losing breath and this could be fatal. Leaving aside all his dreams for personal glory and justification, Kachchua put Cat on his shell. He knew this would reduce his speed to a great extent, but doing this kind act, made Kachchua forget all his ill feelings about the past. All his anger, fear, worry and jealousy vanished into thin air. He knew there was nothing which was more important than a sacred life. He gave his best even with Cat on his back.

He saw Pig coming up behind him. He knew it was only a matter of time, that mouse would be there too. But, it was the last lap wasn't it? Maybe he could still make it. But, this time all his efforts were for Cat. To see to it that she gets help soon. He gave better than his best and could see the finishing line. He raced as fast as he could. Pig was still a few feet behind. Mouse was still not in sight. Kachchua literally ran and ran, forgetting himself, forgetting where and who he was, till he crossed the finishing line.

He quickly signaled the first aid team to help Cat. He then saw that he had in fact come in third last this time! Pig had been just a foot behind him but Mouse was several meters at the back. He was feeling on top of the world! Not only had he managed to save Cat but he had also achieved his dream. The dream was no longer one, where he had to prove anything to himself or to the other animals. He knew that this race did not define who he was. It was decisions like the one he took when he chose to save Cat that were more important and still more important was the fact that he had honored life. By honoring Cat's life, he had honored his own. He saw his true self-worth did not lie in these external pursuits; rather it lay deep within him.

Jackal came panting by. He told the story of how he had gotten trapped in a hunter's net. He had managed to escape, but before escaping he had witnessed Kachchua's selfless act, which had inspired him further, to bite the rope and escape faster. As he caught his breath, he asked everybody to line up for the prize distribution. He mentioned of a special prize this year. The fastest runner would of course get the First Prize, but there was one more prize for the most consistently progressing runner. Jackal gave the First Prize to proud Cheetah, who looked glorious and dashing. For the special prize he announced the winner; Kachchua. Kachchua looked flabbergasted! What? Who? Me? He looked most confused. He looked sheepish and couldn't believe what he was hearing! Jackal then clarified; they had kept a special segment which they had announced only this year, but had been planning it since the last ten years; the most consistent progress of the participants. Every year they measured the speed of each animal. The Cheetah had of course always come in first, but the speed had remained steady at a particular mark. Same was with the other animals. They had remained their regular speed without much improvement or decline. But, with Kachchua, they had witnessed remarkable progress year after year. He kept bettering his own performance with every passing year! This year they had decided that they would give him the prize, even if he came in last.

But, he had really outdone himself this year. As he went up to get the prize, he got a standing ovation! Something even Cheetah had never got. He was so moved to see their love and happiness for him. He had forgotten what it felt like to be loved and to be happy, these last couple of years. So much had he been wallowing in self-pity; tears sprung up in his eyes as he absorbed it all. How wrong he had been. He had had no enemies outside; rather, he himself had been his worst enemy. He now knew that all his insecurities had been in vain, but in some way, he was also thankful to them, for they had got him here; where he was today.

After basking in all the adulation and attention being lavished on him from all directions, Kachchua suddenly remembered Cat. He went to see Cat as he made his way through the crowd. Cat was lying under a tree. He had been attended to and was resting.

Kachchua came up to Cat and asked how he was feeling. Cat was so choked with emotion that he could barely get the words out.

'I'm sorry.......thanks so much..........you are a true Hero, Kachchua......'

'Whoa......what brings this on? I just did what anybody in my place would do. There is no need to thank me and I am most certainly not a hero!'

'Kachchua, for me you will always be a hero. I will never forget this act of love and kindness. I know how much this race meant to you. Why, I was also one among those many who was always teasing you and pulling your leg. I have seen over these years how much you have put into training yourself. For you to sacrifice that race was equivalent to sacrificing life itself. I have no words that can express my gratitude appropriately. Let me just say that I am truly lucky to have you as my friend!'

Suddenly, from being a most useless existence just a few hours ago, Kachchua now felt truly and completely blessed. He admired the trophy he had been given. It was beautiful. He felt silly for feeling the way he had when he would compare himself to others. The jealousy had driven him to where he was today, but he could have gotten here by another method too, which he now knew was the better one. Had he compared himself to his own earlier performance, he could have still achieved this same status, but without all the heartache!

Not one to brood over past mistakes, Kachchua absorbed the learning, let go of his follies, and made his way home. He already knew just the right place where he could display his newly acquired Prize Trophy!

Even after all this time,
The sun never says to the earth,
"You owe me."
Look what happens with
A love like that.
It lights the whole sky.
                              - Hafiz of Persia

Munchy :
The Over-protective Mother Hen

Eight eggs lay in the nest. 'It is time for me to "go broody"', thought Munchy. In hen language that meant that she would stop laying more eggs and now would focus instead on the incubation of these eight eggs. Munchy would barely leave the nest until it was absolutely essential. Just for eating, drinking or dust-bathing would she venture outside; she kept the nest at a steady temperature and humidity as well as turned the eggs over, from time to time. She hated being disturbed and would show her disapproval by protesting and pecking.

This went on for around three weeks after which, one fine morning, Munchy heard faint peeping sounds coming from inside three of the eggs. She knew just as any mother would, that her little babies wanted out. She too made sounds from outside. Clucking, pecking and talking to them in a language only they understood, guiding them to peck the blunt end of the egg, which was at the upper side. They did as guided and soon pecked a hole through the egg.

They were the most adorable sight Munchy had ever seen. Oh, she had seen other newborn chicks but these chicks were extra special. She felt as if she had achieved a wonderful new identity.

She had just participated in the most creative process of life; giving birth to new lives. She felt like God!

She named them Sunny, Softy and Fluffy because they were bright sunny yellow; fluffy; and as soft as cotton balls! She was just so proud to be their mother. She hugged them close and at that very moment such a huge wave of motherly love swept through her, that she decided they were the only priority for her life as of now. There was no other purpose for her existence other than to be their care-giver.

Munchy barely let the chicks out of her sight. For the first couple of weeks it was fine. She would brood them in the nest. Take them out occasionally for food and drink, leading by clucking and feeding them sometimes beak to beak. They loved being around her, so full of love was she; especially Fluffy; he just basked in the attention she gave him. Sunny and Softy would often go out of sight and Munchy would go running after them, to get them back. But, Fluffy liked to be with her. He would not take part in so much of chicking around!

After the first few weeks, Sunny and Softy would want to go out more and more. Munchy grew from being protective and caring to obsessive; 'take care', 'be careful', 'don't hurt yourselves', 'don't talk to strangers', and her instructions and fear got to be the bane of their existence. She would crowd over them at all times. They sometimes felt like they were being suffocated or tied down. They felt they could no more be their regular selves when she was present. Fluffy soon joined in their gang. Now that he was also older, he found more joy with his siblings. He was also starting to find his mother's presence very disturbing. She was constantly on tenterhooks; always shaking with fright, worry or anger. She wanted to dictate everything they did; from the time they got up, till the time they slept. They barely found time to chick around, and whenever they did, she would always be watching with a disapproving look, 'Sunny, be careful, you will hurt Softy!', 'Fluffy, don't play in the sun', 'Softy, take care, you were just about to fall', 'I wonder what you'll would do without me? I am sure you wouldn't last long without my constant vigilance'.

Munchy's paranoia increased day after day. She had nothing else to do. She would watch over the chicks like a watchdog does; always suspicious; worried; concerned; over-protective. She was taking the role of being a mother far too seriously!

The ground shook fiercely under their little feet one day, all of a sudden. Munchy had just gone to the neighboring farm to get some food. The chicks looked at each other, wondering what was happening. A squirrel ran past, the sky is falling! The sky is falling! We are going to die! The ground shook again, more fiercely. The chicks ran to take shelter in the nest. They were not supposed to have gone out. If Munchy got to know about this, they would be in for the worst of it.

The nest was shaking violently. The chicks did not know what to do? Should they stay put or leave the nest as it was starting to get most unstable. They ran and took shelter under the Banyan Tree and were shaking from crown to pointy toe. They were getting terrified by the minute and respite was nowhere in sight. The ground slowly came back to its normal form and there were faint occasional tremors. It was getting calm and they were starting to breathe easy.

Munchy, meanwhile, was cursing herself for leaving her poor helpless chicks behind. What must they be going through? She wondered. This was the first time they were witnessing an earthquake. Munchy had survived two earthquakes before this. Some of her friends hadn't; it had been the time when they were all part of the farm-house. The whole house had collapsed and several of her dear friends had died. She had barely made a close escape and thereafter never lived in a farm-house again. She preferred the open air and free space around her.

As she stood shaking with fear and worry as to what might be happening with her babies,suddenly, a deep sense of knowing came down upon her. She had given her chicks the free life but on the other hand, had stifled their growth because of her own fears, insecurities and worries. Yes, life had been hard on her. But, she was coping pretty well. Life had taught her so many lessons. But, she forgot all that and had started believing as though life for her chicks started with her and ended with her. No, she now realized, life had so much more to offer them. This earthquake coming at the very time when she was not with her chicks was a resounding evidence of the fact that Munchy was not in control. She never had been.

At that time a voice spoke from within, 'they come through you, Munchy, not for you or to you. They are not one of your possessions or trophies. They are your responsibility but not your property. You gave birth which was a great honor for you. But, you forgot that you are not the doer. It is someone else who controls all our strings. We are merely puppets in His hands.'

Surviving, struggling and fighting, was what Munchy had always been doing since the day she was born. Her mother had died at the time of laying eggs. Munchy had not even been properly incubated. She remembered how in the first few weeks of her life, she had always been shaking because of the cold. There had been no one to brood her; to cuddle and peck; to hug and reassure; to love and care.

Munchy had been a survivor. She had been through so many ups and downs in life; that she did not wish to show those days to her chicks, ever. She wanted to be there; to love and care; to hug and reassure; to cuddle and peck.

The bottom line for her had always been, 'I will be there for my chicks. I will not let them be hurt by life's foibles. I will always protect them under my umbrella.'

It had started raining lightly. Munchy stood rooted to the ground. She knew she had to run to her kids. She knew this was when they most needed her. But, her feet wouldn't move. Tears ran down her eyes as she slowly realized the extent to which she had hurt them in trying to save them. How she had stunted their natural growth. How she had succeeded in making bonsais out of banyans.

As all these realizations came crashing down on Munchy, the ground shook lightly once again, the rain showered in bursts and Munchy found herself once more.

'Yay! Mom is back!' screamed Softy, 'Mom, we are here; below the Banyan Tree!'

Munchy walked to her chicks. They came and hugged her so fierce that it brought back new tears to her eyes.

'How are you? Were you really scared? Are you all okay?'

Even though Munchy asked these questions, she just knew they were fine. They then told her how they had been terrified as they did not know what was going on. But, because the three of them were together, they had given each other comfort. They had missed her and wanted her to come back soon.

'I missed you, too, kids. But, I was far away. It took me a while, but I am now back, home. Always remember, you are never alone. The One who has created you, is always with you, even if I am not.'

That day they joyfully made a new home for themselves. It was a warm place where love abided and happiness shone. Munchy's personality had been through a total turnabout. Where at first she had always acted out of fear for her kids, she now acted out of love, knowing that they were being taken care of, by someone other than herself; the One who takes care of us all.

We can make our mind so like still water that beings gather about us to see their own images, and so for a moment live a clearer, perhaps even fiercer life, because of our quiet.

- W. B. Yeats

Pi in the Pea pod

It was a bitterly cold morning when Pi was born upon the earth. It was dark and damp all around. Pi was conscious as Pi for the very first time. She looked around. She was alone. Even through the darkness, Pi gazed all about her with a keen sharp sight. She was surrounded, rather enveloped by a smooth and soft covering; as if to protect her from the cold outside. Pi felt sheltered and safe in her cocoon. She fell back into a deep slumber, feeling loved and secure in her warm surroundings.

Pi was a pea in a pea pod. She was inherently a calm, content and confident pea. She enjoyed life as it unfolded around her. She basked in its' glory and honored every moment of her existence. She considered herself lucky to witness this wonderful creative process called life. She was just so full of gratitude. She thanked her Creator every single day.

This was all before Pi woke up one morning to find herself in the company of a couple more peas in *Her* peapod. "Hey, who are you? What are you guys doing here?" "We are Greenie and Bill. We are your friends. Just arrived….Isn't this place great! What is your name?"

Pi was scandalized! How could somebody invade her home like this? In her confusion she sputtered out, "But how can you just enter my home like this? You have to ask my permission! What if I do not want you here?"

"Hey", Bill replied indignantly, "This is our home too. We were born here when you were sleeping and snoring away like anything."

Pi was confounded. Their home? How could it be? This was her home. Where could she turn? Who could she ask? What could she do? Bill and Greenie, meanwhile, were totally ignorant as to the turmoil in Pi's mind and heart. They looked about in wonder at this wonderful creation called life. They chatted and soon Pi had to turn their chatter into a drone, so that she could think about a solution to this sudden invasion. All the thinking could not bring about a solution, as clearly there was none. She was stuck with their presence, whether she liked it or not.

After the period of bliss, Pi found it difficult to adjust to company. She found their presence stifling and suffocating, not to mention annoying. Couldn't they keep quiet, so that she could think? Chitter chatter all the time! It was getting on her nerves. What would she have to do, to have some quiet time by herself? Just as she was getting adjusted to their being with her, finding quality time for herself when they slept or were at a loss for words, just as she was getting used to them…..

Pi was in for another rude awakening. She discovered three more intruders the next day morning! What is this happening? Oh God, I loved you so much? I believed in you…why are you doing this to me. I do not want all these people here. Please do something. I need my own space to do my own thing (whatever that might be)…….please help me…….."

All around her was chatter chatter. Bickering, arguing, fighting, chatting, laughing, pulling one another's skin, etc. But, one thing it was never, was quiet. Pi had come to like the peace and quiet, in all that time alone. There was only so much she could take! She wanted out. This home did not feel like home anymore. The safe and sheltered cocoon had transformed into a free for all in just a matter of few days! There was no place for Pi. She had been squeezed from both sides and could barely breathe! She forgot all about gratitude, about honoring life and looking at its' beauty. For her, it now seemed that life was unpredictable, terrible and tables could turn at the drop of a hat. Her contentment, calmness and confidence, all went flying out of the peapod! She was losing her patience and peace of mind with every day that passed.

Pi changed. From the quiet and elegant pea that she was. She experienced feelings that she never had before. She did not like them, but what was she to do? Her external space was invaded by the others but her inner sanctuary started being invaded by emotions that were of her own making. She was struggling. Fighting. Lashing out. At life itself. She was putting up resistance. Building walls around herself. She wanted things her way or not at all. She did not realize when she started becoming bitter and sour about everything and everyone around her. She started living in fear. How many more peas would invade her space, she never knew. She was so scared when she opened her eyes in the morning. Pi lived with insecurity. She never was sure what would happen the next moment. She couldn't take any more surprises. She always had her defenses up in case something unappealing were to take place. Pi started worrying and having anxiety. The future looked bleak and full of foreboding. She hated the mornings, noon and night. She hated those around her and herself too for being there.

Her world totally in pieces, not wanting to communicate with anybody, Pi took refuge in the only one thing that made her forget her circumstance. Sleep. She took to sleeping whenever she could. She learned how to drown out the voices, the chatter and all the craziness around her, and went deeper and deeper into a trance like state.

It took some time and practice but she succeeded. She could now be with herself at will. She need not react to everything and everyone around, she learnt. For, if she did not react, things went into a comfortable lull anyway. She found that her fear, worry and insecurity were keeping her from being in the present moment. In these last few days she had only thought about the future with anxiety or pondered on her peaceful past with wistfulness. She had never been truly present to what was. Her fears had seemed to manifest with speed. With her worries increasing, she knew that all that she worried about, soon did come into existence. Her resisting of things gave them birth all the sooner. It now seemed that all her problems were self-created. She was the one inviting trouble into her own life by anticipating them, constantly.

Her struggles, fights and anger had only wounded her. No one else was affected. The only effect it had on the others was that nobody wanted anything to do with her. They all stopped talking to her. Trying to be nice to her. Trying to include her in their conversations. They also started leaving her alone. As she wanted to be. Some of them even looked at her as though she were an alien or something. Somebody in the wrong place at the wrong time. They soon were avoiding her like the plague. It was difficult to do as they were always squished together on both sides. It was the worst of the lot for Greenie and Bill who were the ones on both her sides. She was the one bang in the middle of the pod with four peas on either side!

Till Pi had been the one avoiding and resisting, she had not known how rotten it felt to be the target for such behavior. When the others started behaving that way, she knew what it felt like to be the one at the receiving end. That started making her feel guilty. She regretted and repented her harsh behavior. Pi realized how unreasonable she had been. How selfish and uncaring as to how her attitude was affecting the whole atmosphere in her peapod. They had always been good to her. She had been the one with the problem. She had been the one to initiate trouble, whether her reasons were justified or not.

She would wallow in guilt for days together. How could she change her past? She knew she could not change it. All the time she had wanted alone time. Now, here it was. but, try as she might, she could not wipe out the guilt and shame she seemed to feel. She wanted alone time, yes, but not this way. There was too much negativity in the air now, for her to enjoy peace. Not only were her problems enough, but the other peas had also divided and sub-divided into groups. Fights and arguments were the order of the day.

No love and respect was left in the peapod between any two peas. They all were unsure about the others. They had all built walls around themselves and resisted each other. They doubted and feared. Worried and fought. It was becoming terrible.

Pi wished to disappear or die. She did not want to be here anymore. No doubt that at the back of her mind, she knew that she was the one who had started this.

Had it not been for her, they would probably all be living as happy peas in a pod.

This realization really woke Pi up. She stopped moping around. She took charge of her mind and feelings again. She was determined to make things better. She knew that a way would soon be shown to her by her Creator. She had messed things up by not trusting and having faith in what was. In resisting the process. She would now patch things up by giving all her problems to the one who was her Creator. Surely he would be the only one who could now get her out of this mess. She would have to trust him and trust what would be shown. She would have to develop the keen sight that had been hers when she had been born. She would have to work to bring the positive outlook once again into her life. She had been born with little needs and desires. Her circumstances had changed her but she was aware that if she really wanted to, she could change once again. She would have to change to bring peace back into her heart.

Now, this time, she did not give in to an escape such as sleep. Rather, she learnt the art of quietening her mind. Even if chaos prevailed around her, she could be calm within. She learnt the art of being with herself in peace with all the chattering and bickering around her. It did not affect her inner space like before. She was clearing up cobwebs of her self-created chaotic past. She was constantly opening herself to a universe other that the small peapod. She even became aware of sounds from outside. The sunrise and sunset were known to her. The moonlight was one thing she basked in. She loved the breeze as it gently caressed the pod and swung them to sleep. She discovered the joy of being alive once more. She would now talk to her neighbors with a bright smile in her voice. She began to respect their being. She would bring awareness to them too, of the outside world as well as the beauty of the inner world. As she grew, so did they. Bill and Greenie were her best friends now, but Pi was friendly with all of them. How big hearted of them to have forgiven her obnoxious behavior so easily. They had begun a new journey with a clean slate and everyone had agreed to harmonize the atmosphere as no one liked it so negative. They were all fun loving peas with good pure intentions in their hearts.

Pi taught them the art of alertness and awareness. As grew Pi, so grew all the peas in the pod. It was another cold bitter morning, when Pi went into a trance like state. Everybody was sleeping in the pod. Pi grew aware of the breathing. Her breathing. Bill breathing. Greenie breathing. All of them breathing. The peapod breathing. The whole plant breathing. As Pi grew in her awareness, Pi was just Pi no more. Pi was Bill. Pi was Greenie. Pi was all the others. Pi was the peapod. She was the whole plant. She was the air. She was the soil. She was the water in the air and the soil. Pi was the cloud. Pi was the bird. Pi was the sun. Pi was one with all.

As Pi opened her eyes after a long time, she was full of love for all and one.

The pod opened up.........Pi fell out along with the others............ they soon merged back into the earth.........coming or going........ one could not say..........

One needs something to believe in, something for which one can have whole-hearted enthusiasm. One needs to feel that one's life has meaning, that one is needed in this world.

- Hannah Senesh

Pitara and the Illusion of Space

Pitara an earthen pot was the regular water carrier in the Mishra household. Sakshi, the daughter of Mr. Mohanlal Mishra, would carry Pitara between her arm and hip when she went down to the river, to fill him to the brim with pure river water. Pitara was proud of himself for being so useful to his family. He loved it when they were satisfied as they drank water and quenched their thirst because of him. He doted on the attention he got as he was being cleaned and taken care of.

Pitara had lived all his life here. He was very much a part of their family. Mr and Mrs Mishra, Sakshi and Soham loved him a lot. He too loved them with all his heart. He served them with all his soul. He was happy when they were happy. He was sad when they were sad.

Then, one day the unthinkable happened. Sakshi was preoccupied with some thoughts and tripped on a stone. She fell and bruised her knees and Pitara wished sincerely that she was not hurt, even though he was in pain himself, as he had hurt his sides. Sakshi bravely got up as well as picked him up. He was in such agony as he had never experienced before. But, he put on a brave front. Sakshi continued to the river and as usual started doing her job.

As she started back, she saw that the pot was emptying itself out. She filled him again and once again the water was running out as fast as it could. She turned Pitara from all sides and tried to see what was wrong. 'Oh no,' thought Sakshi, 'there is a crack here!'

She turned to go back home and braced herself for a scolding.

'It is okay, Sakshi, you fell and the pot broke. It is no big deal. Just put it in the store-room and I will get another one in a while. I hope you haven't hurt yourself. Let me see…hold still, Sakshi…', said Sakshi's mother, Fulwa.

Pitara lay in a corner of the hall; nobody as much as glanced at him. He was in deep pain, physically and now emotionally too. He had been discarded with not a moment's hesitation! He thought he was family; he had served them all his life; and now this step-pot treatment was too much to bear. Fulwa picked him up after she attended to Sakshi's bruise. She did not even bother to see where he had hurt himself. She walked out of the house to the store-room outside and left him there in a dingy corner.

One moment he had been at the peak of his glory and the next…..in the dirtiest place he had ever seen. It was true, he thought, about the glitter and glory all being transient! He had thought all those things only happen to other pots. He had thought that such a thing could never happen to him. He had been so disillusioned by their love and care. But, all that, he knew now, was only till he could be of any use to them. Once his usefulness was gone, so was their love.

Pitara found all this overwhelming and unknowingly went into a depressive state. He would lie all day, feeling morose and unhappy. He did notice though that he was the only one there in such a state. Everyone else was reasonably cheerful and chirpy. He resisted their friendship for a while but soon succumbed and loosened up. There were a few more pots and pans, some bedding and bedcovers, pillows and other discarded stuff. They spoke to each other as they had no other form of entertainment. They would crack jokes and they even made one about Pitara, calling him a 'cracked pot'!

His self-obsession decreased day after day, as he saw the unity amongst the diversity here. He was no longer the special one who served his dear family. He was now a common pot that lay after its usefulness was depleted. He still hurt at times but as they say, time is the greatest healer. So was the case with Pitara. He healed and helped others heal too as they discovered fresh new aspects to their personalities.

Pitara adjusted to his newly found freedom pretty soon and his Mishra household days were a faint memory of the past! One day, as luck were to have it, a cat got into the store-room. She had just given birth to kittens and needed a safe place where they would not be disturbed. As the newest member of this room, Pitara was reasonably cleaner than the other objects and the cat seemed drawn to him. She carefully placed her kittens inside Pitara and left to get them some food.

Pitara once again found a reason to be full of joy! He was being of some service again. He was so happy and thanked God for this new duty that had come by on its own. His pot space was being useful once more. It was like a second life for Pitara. God had given him one more chance. He was deeply grateful for all he had in life.

Days went by as Pitara served his new owners; the cat and her kittens. They loved him just as much as he loved them. They would tickle his belly as they played pranks on each other and bickered as only two siblings could. Pitara overlooked all this like a fond parent. This time round, even though Pitara had to keep reminding himself, he was careful to protect himself. There was an invisible wall around Pitara that would allow nothing past it. Not even the endearing kittens, though they did get pretty close. He cared but with a watchfulness. He loved but with a sense of self-preservation.

One day the squabble took a serious turn and the kittens were not fighting so innocently any longer. They were scratching each other with a menace and screaming so loud that it was deafening! Before Pitara knew what was happening, Fulwa came in to see what the commotion was about. As she set her eyes on Pitara, her mouth curled itself into a scowl, and she came charging at him with a stick in her hands!

'No! No!' screamed Pitara, but his screams fell on deaf ears. Before he knew it, life as Pitara was over for him. Fulwa had broken him to pieces and was now busy getting rid of the kittens. Pitara lay there feeling miserable and dead. Life was over! It was the end of the world for him...

As he lay there, in pieces, Pitara wondered why he could still think and feel. He was dead, wasn't he? Why did all this hurt so much? Could this be possible once you die? Pitara then found that he was floating. He was still there even though all his walls had been killed. Even though he lay there like a mutilated corpse. Pitara found that not only was he still there, but that he was a part of everything. He was the other pot, the bedding, the bedcover; he was the pan and the fan; he was the floor and the roof; he was the wall as well as the space between the walls!

Pitara was delighted to find out that he was not dead! He was truly alive for the first time in his life! He did not feel the need to serve any longer. He was providing the biggest service to all; being the substratum where all and nothing existed;

He realized he was the sky as well as the earth. He was the wind as well as the fire. He was in everything and everything was in him. All the previous hurt, confusion and walls gave way as Pitara found that he was not Pitara, He was space! All of it! And then he realized an even greater truth. Everybody can have this awareness. The only reason they do not is, because they tend to give too much importance to their smaller selves, their bodies, their walls, just as he had. If we can break through this barrier after we are dead, we can break through it even when alive. It is only a matter of seeing differently! This feeling of infinite vastness, unending bliss is not only for him…it is for one and all!

Pitara discovered his true nature:

'I am space. I just am. Everything and everybody are in me. I am everywhere. I am the beginning and the end but I have no beginning or end. I am the alpha and the omega. I am The thing everybody is after. But, no one thinks that they are after me, unfortunately.

I am the expanse of infinity which is the birthright of even the tiniest speck on earth. Everybody can be Me, only that no one knows it yet.

Once you are Me, all the chase comes to an end; the pursuit of happiness, success, name, fame, prosperity and heck, even enlightenment, seeing God, etc., come to an end once you experience Me. But a box thinks it is just a box and feels the need to compete with other boxes. Size, shape, color and quality all become the most important things for him.

A rose thinks it is merely a rose. It tries to outshine the other roses by enhancing its color, fragrance and beauty. A cow thinks it is just a cow. It merely eats, drinks and sleeps. A human thinks of himself as just a human: a combination of body, mind, intellect and soul.

I thought of myself as only a pot, but now I know that I was conditioned that way because of my body, the pot. The space that carried the water in me, as Pitara, was not separate from the total space. It was just that I gave too much of importance to being Pitara. The space that gave shelter to the kittens was no different from the space outside the store-room. But, alas, I never knew my own presence.

Everybody is content just being their own conditioned selves, when they can be so much more. They forget or rather have forgotten that they all were space once. Not just a part of it. But, It. They all knew what it feels like to be the expanse of infinity. But as we love playing games, this game of life is played by one and all. Everyone are so engrossed in the game, they are enjoying the playing of the game so much, that they forget this is just that, a game. I can now see from this viewpoint the futility of our lives till we believe ourselves to be limited by names and forms.

We forget the Reality and become part of the unreal.

The box which is smaller and ugly competes with the big attractive box, not remembering that they are one and the same, from where they came originally. They think of themselves as only the box, because they have identified themselves to be only that. The rose is not just the rose. It is everything. It contains everything as it contains life. Whether it competes or doesn't compete, till it thinks of itself as just a rose, it is not living life to its full glory and honor.

A human can be so much more! They can do more, other than competing, struggling, fighting, resisting, constricting their own growth, arguing, pushing away love, looking for happiness in all the wrong places! They are given the greatest gift. They are given the gift of choosing: how to live, think and feel.

It all began when all were me and I was all. Then 'one' got the idea that it was someone other than me, the 'whole'. He thought he was better than Me and went his separate way, which is still within Me, but he thinks it is not. Then he instigated others to go along with him and thus this sorry state has come to be, that they all have forgotten Me. Some find their way back, some stay, some get lost again. Some never find their way simply because they don't feel like changing themselves.

I wait. I keep waiting. I witness. I keep watching silently. I am always awake. I never sleep. I am awareness itself. I am life itself. I know all will find their way back someday, for that is their destiny, their legacy. But, each will do it at their own speed. For each has their free-will. I do not push anyone. I am not desperate, though I do feel nice when someone makes their way back. Each will do it when they are ready, when their time has come: and it will, of that one thing I am sure! Just as it came for Pitara … It did.......'

Our deepest fear is not that we are inadequate. Our deepest fear is that we are powerful beyond measure. It is our light, not our darkness that most frightens us. We ask ourselves, 'Who am I to be brilliant, gorgeous, talented, fabulous?' Actually, who are you not to be?

You are a child of God. Your playing small does not serve the world. There's nothing enlightened about shrinking so that people won't feel insecure around you. We are meant to shine, as children do. We were born to make manifest the glory of God that is within us. It's not just in some of us: it's in everyone.

And as we let our own light shine, we unconsciously give other people permission to do the same. As we're liberated from our own fear, our presence automatically liberates others.

-Marianne Williamson in A Return to Love

Sesam Blossoms

"*Ooh!! This light is blinding! What is this place? Where am I? It is so bright that I cannot see anything. I have been in the dark for far too long! It will take time to get accustomed to this light.....*"

Life had been a constant struggle and fight for Sesam, the lotus bud, up until now. It had been phases of fight, flight and living a fearful and disgusted existence. Struggles external and struggles internal. Cursing the dreary and unfavorable surroundings had become practically customary for Sesam, but there were also times that he cursed his own fate, his very being, his existence itself and he did not forget to curse his creator, who had put him here in the first place.

The muck around him suffocated him. He found it difficult to breathe. It was not a rare sight to see tears falling down his face as he gave in to the weakness and helplessness he so often felt. He just did not know what to do! He was this tiny life and the problems facing him were monumental.

In between these stormy moments, came times of peace and calm, too; when he felt confident about himself. Though these were few and far between, they were there. At times like these Sesam communicated with higher forces that could not be seen, only felt. The feeling Sesam got at these times was full of warmth, acceptance and love. The only message he instinctively got was that he had to 'wait'. He was told telepathically that there was a purpose in even the worst of scenarios and that his time would come. Sesam would not be satisfied by this. He would ask, 'But how, but when.......why.......but.......' There were no more answers. No more messages. That was all. The higher forces too deserted his never-ending onslaught of questions. They could only give one more message very firmly. 'Have faith'. And so the cycle would go on.

Sesam would get up in the morning, not feeling fresh, never looking forward to the day ahead. He would desolately look around him. There was a variety of other plants and beings around him. They looked beautiful and happy. Satisfied and content with their lot. Sesam would often wonder, 'Am I in the wrong place? Am I here by mistake? I think there has been a huge error because I do not feel like I fit in here!' He would scream internally, 'Let me out! I don't belong here! Please take me to where I really belong!', would be his desperate plea. He was full of conviction that this was not his true place. He was not meant to be here. It was the work of some twisted humor that had got him here. A cruel joke that life had played on him!

The problem was that there was no one to listen. No one to understand. No one who could relate to his feelings. Nobody could help.

After a few weeks Sesam did what anybody in his place would have done; he starting adjusting; to the muck; to the smells; to the stuffy feeling; to the weakness and helplessness. He started accepting this as his destiny. He opened up and became friendly with a few plants nearby. While these conversations and communications helped him forget his troubles, at times they created further unendurable troubles for him; putting him deeper into the dumps. At these times Sesam felt like he was all alone in the whole world! He wished the mucky ground would swallow him up and make life easier by putting him to death!

But, it was at these times alone, when he got closer to a new friend; a friend who spoke to him in his mind; through his thoughts. He knew this was not his own voice for his own voice had never ever communicated with such love and compassion. It had almost always condemned him and put him down. This other friendly voice encouraged him, prodded him on, showed him a positive image of things and always invariably made him feel better. One day it told him to be alert to his surroundings. Not to be so lost in self-pity that he could not see clearly what all went around him.

Sesam realized that whenever he was lost in his thoughts, he would not only start feeling lower than he already was, but he could never be normal with others around him. He would behave crabby and irritated. It seemed like Sesam loved being miserable. He had created a parallel world with his thoughts where he was the victim. He loved that sorry world so much that he escaped into it every now and then. He would not like being roused from this world when others wanted him to do or say something else.

When the voice told him to 'be alert', it had come as quite a surprise. What was there to be alert about. What could be different? What could be new here? He felt as if he now knew everything. Yet the voice was confident. So Sesam looked around. Everything looked the same; the same muck; the same plants and weeds; the same beings floating around; everybody content. No, nothing was different. It was all the same as before.

Sesam asked the voice, 'What do I have to be alert for? It all looks the same and frankly speaking, the content look on these faces makes me sick. They hammer in the fact that I am like a square peg in a round hole. I feel better being miserable with my thoughts than being miserable looking around and trying to fit in somewhere in my environment.'

'Be alert', was all the voice would say again. 'The time will come when your alertness will get you what you desire.'

And so, time ticked away and Sesam slowly and steadily learned the art of 'being present', 'being alert' and 'being here'. It had been painful to extract himself from the web of thoughts he had become so used to living in. It had become a habit. He had adjusted. And just when he was happy in his own sorrow, the 'be alert' signals were being given! Anyway, Sesam endured the pain till the day he came to enjoy the feeling of being present in the here and now. It was as though he was miraculously given a new set of eyes. A new way of *seeing*! And so Sesam developed *clarity*. He became *patient* and most importantly, he developed a strong *will*, a *positive attitude* and started *having faith* in the friendly voice.

The turnaround came for Sesam one day when he woke up feeling great and as usual took in his surroundings. It shocked him to see someone just like himself. What was all the more shocking and hurtful was that this someone was in a much higher place! 'What is that? Who is that?', asked Sesam to a neighboring friend. 'That is someone just like you', came the quick reply. 'B..but how did he get so high up? I have always been here!' The friend merely shrugged and slithered away, leaving Sesam fuming.

Sesam demanded the voice to explain to him what was going on. He was indignant and felt cheated. It was more like he had been stabbed in the back or stem or something. The voice replied a wee bit too slowly, 'Sesam, you too can go higher. My friend, you never tried. From the day you were born, you have cursed yourself, curled up and willed to die, constricted and restricted your growth. Now, that is exactly where you are.' Sesam realized the truth in these words with great pain. He understood that it had always been in his own hands. No one else was responsible. Not the muck. Not the content plants and beings he had cursed. No. It had always been himself. As it turned out, he had succeeded in becoming his own worst enemy. He had wasted his life away. The voice knew that Sesam would once again go into the Great Depression if he didn't take control. So, the voice was gentle and loving with his next words, 'All is not lost, Dear Sesam. It is not the end of the world. You still have time. There is always time after the *knowing*. Choice is in our hands. You cannot undo the past but you can create your own tomorrow. *Choose* to do that. All you have to do is do the exact opposite of what you have always been doing. Expand yourself and see new horizons! Go for it, Sesam!'

It was not easy. Taking life transforming decisions never is. But the *deciding* to do this gave him confidence and strength. Taking the decision and choosing a different path got the ball rolling. One thing led to the other. It was like he was being carried by the universe itself. He was buoyant. He was floating and he was free of all the limitations he had imposed on himself! Sesam let down all the mental guards he had put up in an effort of conserving himself. As the guards were down, the vibrancy of pure emotion led Sesam to feel a vibration in each and every cell of his body. Sesam felt so full of positive energy. He had never felt this way before. He now had *direction* in his life. He knew he was meant to go higher.

So began a new phase of Sesam's life. Every day in every way, this is what he did. He *desired* to go higher. He *saw* himself going higher. He *felt* himself going higher. He had *faith* that he was going higher. He asked his cells to *help* him. He took daily *guidance* from the friendly voice. He asked God to give him *strength, energy and vitality.*

One day, Sesam awoke feeling different. He looked around and noticed things around him were different too. He looked below, something he had never done! Lo and behold!! Sesam was in the air. He had shot up into the air. Sesam was overjoyed. All his hard work had finally paid up! Witnessing this feat was miraculous to Sesam and he felt on top of the world. He knew now for certain that he was on the *right path*. He felt like singing and dancing and announcing his achievement to the whole world! He had never known such a *happy* day in all his life! Then something strange happened! He felt a warm tingly feeling all over his body. It was delicious and made Sesam feel good all over. 'What is this sensation?' Sesam asked the friendly voice. The voice quipped, 'This is *love*, Sesam. You have shown true faith to the universe and it is showering you with true love. You have always been truly loved, Sesam, but the power to feel it, accept it, honor it and rejoice in it were missing in you, up until now. Your time, as I promised, is here. Savor this experience to the full and bask in its glory, Sesam. This is your moment.'

Sesam felt glorious. He allowed this feeling to take over his mind and body; his heart and soul. He floated with it. He reveled in it. All of this had always been his *legacy*. Only he had doubted it from the very beginning. It had only been a matter of time.

Sesam was confused about one thing though. He wondered why he had been so low and down in the dumps for so long. Why no one else around him seemed to be in that state. He voiced his confusion, 'Does everyone go through the pain to come to this place?' 'No, Sesam, not everyone has the same experience. It is different for everyone. This experience was meant for you. Each one is special in their own way. Each has different lessons to learn. We never hold it if one does not make it. But, with each step that you do, the universe rejoices in your joy. Some take years to learn. Some learn quick with hardly any pain. But, we have faith that each one will get there, sooner or later. 'But, what happened to me? Why was I miserable for so many days? I feel cheated out on time….'

'You lose more time if you look back with regret. What you went through back then is what brought you here. Don't play the blame game anymore as that will once again constrict your growth. The past is gone. Let it go. Learn from it what you will. Learn and do not repeat the same mistakes. You lived in fear, you lashed out at the world in a survival mode. You hated your surroundings. You closed yourself. You hampered your growth. Now, what is the difference? Love has happened. Where fear exists, love cannot. Where love is, fear has no holding. But, it is not that once you have experienced love, fear will never touch you again. No. Fear creeps back the second you are not aware. So, Sesam, even after achieving these great heights, you could fall back to the same state you were in, if you lose your *awareness*. Be very careful. Be alert; all the time; after all, Sesam. I am a part of you. I am your voice; nobody else's. Yes. You were not aware before. You thought I was someone else and I let you go on thinking that way. But, I am your voice only. You have two voices; one, based on fear, which will make you lash out at the world, which will let you wallow in self-pity; the one who loves misery. The one who loves making you feel like the victim. I am your second voice. The one you hardly ever heard because you liked listening to the other voice. You pushed me away and then my words were a mere chatter in the background. But I never left your side, Sesam. I was harsh at times and what I told you to do was difficult. But, it was only based on love that I did all that. I am the voice that is always based on love. You listened too, when all else failed. Sometimes, it is at the brink of the destruction of our very being, that we listen to the voice of love. So it was with you, that the times when you felt all else was lost, were the very times that you could communicate with me. But, just because your communications with me have become clearer and easier, it does not mean that the other voice has been destroyed. No. That voice will always be with you, just as I will. You will have to be alert and aware. Your choices and decisions will shape your tomorrow.'

Sesam was astounded as to what was required out of him. A constant surveillance of his own thoughts! Would he be able to do it? Yes, he knew with an inner certainty that we could and that he would. He had gone through the worst phase and come out winning. This was a cinch after that. He knew he needed constant guidance. He mentally thanked his inner voice and once again began the process of seeing, believing, feeling and knowing that he was going higher and higher; as grew his conviction, so grew his height.

The day was not far when Sesam broke through the surface and saw the *light*. It was like emerging after a long and deep slumber. A few moments of blinding light and then it had been the most beautiful experience of Sesam's life. The world was a great place to be in.

Sesam blossomed into a pretty pink lotus feeling the deep love and acceptance of the universe....

Most people can look back over the years and identify a time and place at which their lives changed significantly. Whether by accident or design, these are the moments when, because of a readiness within us and a collaboration with events occurring around us, we are forced to seriously reappraise ourselves and the conditions under which we live and to make certain choices that will affect the rest of our lives.

- Frederick F. Flack

The Story of Coca- A Small Fish

This is my story. My name is Coca. I am a small clownfish in the ocean. I am alone. There are other fish close by. But in my home, my anemone, I am alone. I have friends but I feel I am different. I love them and they love me but I still feel different because they all seem to be very happy with their lives. They are totally engrossed in their little homes, their day to day activities and their routines. I want to be like them. But, no, I am haunted by questions day in and day out.

"Why am I so small?"

"Why am I so scared of big fish?"

"How cruel is the creator who created this world full of big fish eating up the smaller fish! If he did have to make such vastly different sizes, shouldn't he have provided different food for them?"

"Not only do they eat smaller fish but they do not even give a seconds thought to it."

"Why does this world have to be survival of the fittest? Shouldn't everybody be well provided for?"

"How come the strong have a hold over the weak and why is the destructive/negative always got a higher fin over the constructive/positive?"

Funny things happen to me when I see particular sights. When I see a big fish eat smaller fish, I feel two things happening. I feel very weak and helpless because I can do nothing to save the smaller fish. This makes me angry with myself. And I feel anger towards the bigger fish for being so nonchalant about it! I hate this feeling. This getting angry, feeling weak and helpless, being terrified that I might be their next meal if they spot me. I am tired of hiding. I want to be free from this fear. What should I do? When I sleep at night I am even scared that I might never wake up again.

Then again, my friends wonder why I am not eating smaller fish than myself. I used to, in the beginning. Then I would feel guilty! Why did I eat a helpless fish? I would say to myself. Then I found that eating plants and weeds was easier on my conscience than eating a live fish. So, I turned vegetarian.

Anyway, getting back to the questions that are driving me crazy. And these thoughts and feelings. I am quite literally going out of my mind! Why can't I be like everyone else. I feel so envious of them. They really do have a good grasp over their lives. They are happy. They don't care about all these things. They are not being haunted by all these questions.

Why? Why?

How? How?

One night I could take it no more. My friend was the one who was eaten up that day. I was missing him and the questions came back with a vengeance. I once again felt helpless as the onslaught began and this time I could not tolerate it. What was the meaning of this life? What was it that my creator wanted me to do? What did he want me to learn? Which message was I not getting? I was tired and weary of this painfully fearful existence. The feelings made me feel very rotten and I felt something that I had never felt before. I cursed life. I felt like my living had no meaning. I cursed the creator. I cursed myself. I cursed everybody and anybody, everything and anything. I did not want to live anymore. I neither understood life nor its mysteries.

I fell asleep, rather, I cried myself to sleep without the fear of whether I would wake up or not. As I slept I had a wonderful dream. I was in a beautiful place. In all my travels to exotic locations, I had never come across such a place. There were majestic mountains, tall trees, birds chirping sweetly in the distance and I was in a clear, sparkling, crisp running stream. The water life was so colorful. The corals were such as I have never seen before. The other fish in the stream were unlike my old friends. The sun shining down on the water was much brighter and warmer. This place seemed to be from another planet altogether! In fact it seemed like I had traveled out of this world!

Then I heard the most loving voice I have ever heard! The voice was soothing, caressing. It seemed to envelope me in its warmth. It took me a while to realize that the voice was talking to me.

"Why are you sad, little one?"

Here in this wonderful place was someone asking me this question for the very first time. For, I generally did not show my feelings in front of others. At least not these deep, personal feelings. These were private. Nobody knew and nobody wanted to know. But, now all of a sudden, there was somebody so concerned! Really, genuinely concerned.

When did the dam burst? Before I knew it, my lifelong unanswered questions just came pouring out. All my doubts, fears, frustrations, anger, confusion. Everything.

The questions I had never asked anybody. The questions I hated. The questions I wanted to put inside a shell and bury so deep within the seabed, that they would never surface ever again. Some which even I didn't remember. From a time of long ago. When I was in a different place. Around fish who did not love me and I did not love them. Even those surfaced, which took me totally by surprise. The questions that I thought I had forgotten. All of them were finding their way out.

"Why are fish so selfish?"

"Does common courtesy mean nothing to others?"

"How can fish be so self-centered that another's pain and hurt does not affect them at all?"

"Why is everyone always grabbing and never giving?"

"Why do fish have to be so rude? Can they not say the same thing nicely?"

"Fish can be really mean!"

"Is this struggle all that life means? Do we have to be constantly going against the stride?"

"When is this going to get better?"

"When will I be happy?"

"Where can I find love?"

"When will I be rid of these thoughts and feelings that make me feel bad?"

And they went on and on..............

As the questions slowed I finally asked, "What should I do? I cannot live with myself anymore. I think it will be better that a big fish make me his next meal!"

The voice asked, "Coca, answer this honestly. I say honestly because, if you are not honest with yourself, you will never be honest to yourself. So, tell me. Do you love yourself?"

Indignantly and reasonably so, I replied, "Of course! What a question!"

"How do you know you love yourself?" persisted the voice.

"Well, I just know it!" I was still indignant.

"OK. How many times a day do you put yourself down? Are you not too harsh on yourself? Do you not have too many expectations from yourself, and do you not berate yourself when you do not live up to those expectations?" asked the voice.

"Uh! Quite often I guess" my voice not indignant anymore.

"Is that how you express your love?"

"No. No."

"How do you show your love to others?"

"Well, I accept them for what they are, which is sometimes not easy, but when I really love someone, acceptance just comes. There are times when I do not understand them, but I still accept them. I love them for being 'them'."

"So, do you love yourself for being 'you'?"

"No. Not really. I am hardly ever happy with myself. I always want to please everybody. I want to do more and more all the time. In the process, nor do I please others, nor do I please myself, nor do I do what I have to do just for the joy of doing it. Now that you ask me, the joy of doing things just for the sake of the joy, is gone. I seem to be doing things, because, either I have to do it, I am supposed to do it, it is my job to do it, if I don't do this what will the other fish think and say etc etc. You just made me realize that the 'joy' element has disappeared from my life! Another thing to be sorry for. Why did this have to happen to 'me'? Why do I always get the short end of the stick? Why is 'my' life so miserable? Is my creator taking out some personal revenge on me? Is this some punishment I am going through for some past sins? Why is what I do never good enough? Why can I not 'be' myself in front of others? Why doesn't anybody understand me? Why am I a square peg in a round hole? When will I fit in? Am I a misfit? Is something wrong with me?"

Oh Oh the dam was bursting again! What was this? Every thought seemed to be a stimulant for a series of queries! Long forgotten times were coming to the surface again. What was happening this night? I did not want to relive painful memories of the times from when I was with fish who did not love me and I did not love them.

I had hidden them deep within me. How come they were coming back now? When I already had so much to deal with. Could they not remain within the deep recesses of my heart?

The voice went on speaking as it knew not the state of my heart. "Do you want me to help you?"

"I think I am beyond any help now. I'll just have to go to La La Land or someplace like that where there are a few others like me." I said in despair.

"Nobody is ever beyond any help. Help is always at hand. You only have to ask for it. Ask and it is there. Do you trust me? Do you really have faith in me?"

"Yes. I think I do."

"All these words, 'try, maybe, I think', are not worthy of being used often. 'Try' generally means you never will. 'Maybe' generally means no. And 'I think' is very vague. It means you are not full of conviction. You are not sure. Not being sure means having doubt. When there is doubt, faith can never be there. So, are you sure?"

"Yes. I trust you. In fact, right at this moment, I entrust my life to you. I surrender to you, body and soul. My life is mine no more. I am in your fins now. Do with me what you will."

"OK. That is a good start. Now, I want you to accept yourself. You are here for a particular reason. A particular purpose. There are no extras here. Are you willing to accept yourself, quirks or no quirks, wholly and completely?"

This question took a little longer to answer. The memories haunting me were coming back with a fierce vengeance. The fish who did not love me had given my 'being' a great beating. I had not always been like this. They used to criticize me, laugh at me, put me down constantly, were always unhappy with what I did, always corrected me, till a time came that I felt I was good for nothing. If I ate, they told me this was not the right way for eating. I should do it 'their' way. If I helped in chores, they told me this was not 'their' way of doing chores. I had to change myself to please them at every step of my way. Everything and anything I did was wrong. If I did not change, I was not accepted. If I changed, and I did, I was still not accepted, and to top that, I started to slowly forget who I was originally. The Coca I was got lost somewhere in that place around those fish who did not love me. Coca got lost and vanished so, that I could not find him, even when I left that place. After having left that place since a couple of years, I am still searching for him. So, can I accept myself as this broken down personality when I have known a fuller and more complete one? How can I do that when I know that this 'me' is just a fragment of what I truly was. But, I now realize from this place of wisdom, just being with this wise voice, that it was never their fault. They were never wrong in what they did. The fault had always been mine. If I had loved myself this would never have happened. If I had faith in myself and my creator, this would not have happened. I was the one who gave my power to them. I showed them that they could alter my personality, leaving me broken and clueless. Why had I not loved myself. Why had I always felt like I am not good enough. How then, could I blame them for not loving me? How could I blame them for not accepting and understanding me, for I have never accepted and understood myself. Till this moment, I had never really thought about all these things. A pandora's box had opened up and there was no slowing down. There was no backing out. I would have to face my ghosts. I would have to resolve the past if I wanted a brighter future. I would have to learn new things, in new ways which would not always be a bed of roses. Inevitable pain seemed to come up like a wall in front of my eyes.

The voice had another great quality. It was so patient. It never prodded me to answer immediately. It just waited. And the funnier thing was, without the voice having said much, I felt much better, I was seeing things more clearly. Answers too seemed to be coming out from within me, not just questions. I was having so many insights on this journey, it was fascinating.

"See, many experiences have made me bitter. They have broken my personality. I am not sure if I can turn the clock back, in a minute, just like that." I was honest in voicing my self-doubt.

"Time is only in your mind. Doubt is only in your mind. The experiences made you bitter because you were too ready to accept that you are not good enough. They affected you so deeply because you never loved and accepted the true glory of who you are. There is one part of our minds that is always easily willing to accept the worst of ourselves. It thrives on pain. It thrives on self doubt. It thrives on being stuck in a situation from which it does not have to make an effort to get out of. The mind does not like change. But, sweet Coca, change is life. If we don't change, we stagnate, and I'm telling you, the mind likes that. It can control you only when you are weak and it is powerful. When we flow with our unreasonable feelings, react immediately to them, we are giving the rein to the mind. If you want to hold the rein of your mind, it will require effort, maybe pain. It will require thinking. Contemplation. Introspection. And along with these, focusing on higher qualities is the key. Remember love, happiness and peace rather than crying about the pain, anger, fear.

We can only overcome the lower by not wallowing in that but by leaping out of it with a focus on faith, love and happiness. These qualities will not be affected by being around those who love you or those do not love you. The only important thing is for you to love yourself. There is a deep place within where love, happiness and peace abide. We can get to that place with focus and intent. Awareness and understanding. Not by being stuck where we are and crying. You can get to that place when you understand that happiness is not about whether the big fish ate the small fish or not. Happiness is not about whether you could save your friend or not. Happiness just 'is'. It already exists. It is 'covered' with your veils of 'why' and 'how'. Remove the veils and you will 'dis' 'cover' happiness, peace and love.

Do not condemn the questions. They are what got you here. But, think again. Is this the only place you want to stay. For if you do not change, you stagnate. So, you need not condemn any part of your life, any part of your experience. You need not curse life, the creator, yourself, others. You just need to accept. Every part of it. for it made you who you are today. Had it not been for all this, would you be in this special place, where only a few select fish get to travel to? So, tell me, can you accept yourself, wholly and completely. With all the pain. All the confusion. All the fears and anger. All the past. All the condemning and judging? Can you?"

"Yes. I can."

"Then it takes only a fraction of a second. Just close your eyes. Tell yourself these few things. 'I love myself. I accept myself. I am beautiful.' This will change your attitude about yourself which will then help you to change your attitude, outlook and expectations from the world. See it all boils down to what choice we make. What decisions we take. What we are today is nothing but our choices and decisions of the past. What we will be tomorrow will be a result of the choices and decisions that we make or take today. The mind is very fickle. It will control you but the moment you tell your mind your final decision firmly, it has no choice but to give in. You become the master of your mind once, and each time it squeezes back in to overthrow your power, it will become easier and easier, to not let it succeed."

"I accept myself wholly and completely from this moment on. But, what you are saying about mind and control is beyond my capacity! I cannot understand all this."

"See, Coca, it is actually pretty simple. Today, you are a fearful, angry and frustrated existence because of the choices and decisions you took in the past. Tomorrow if you wish to be strong, happy, healthy and confident, it will require making better choices and decisions. What you make your life to be is your choice. You have the final word and no one else. You are not just a creature of circumstance. You are your circumstance. You need to feed yourself love and acceptance, but the real key is to change your attitude and outlook about life and other fish. When you wake up, it is going to be the same world out there. It depends on you, do you want to react or do you want to act? There will be the same big fish eating the small fish. Strength and power will have the upper fin against the weak and down-trodden. Nothing or nobody outside of you will change. What will change is your perception. Your reaction. Your attitude. Your inner world will change. Something deep deep inside will turn over. It will give way to the new and get rid of the old. You will see the world with new eyes. Where you will not be angry with the big fish for eating the small fish for you will understand that that is what they 'are'. You will not feel helpless when this happens though you may feel compassion for the small fish because you will understand that this is what their life 'was'. You may not want to eat smaller fish than yourself, even now, because that is who you 'are' and if a big fish were to eat you tomorrow, you will know that this is what your life was meant to 'be'.

But, whatever happens, you will most certainly not ever feel fear again. Because you are now surrendered to me. You have faith in me. You trust me and I am always by your side, though you cannot see or feel me. Where there is faith, there is no place for fear, doubt or confusion. If you go about your life, accepting and loving yourself unconditionally, facing life with courage, commitment, confidence and compassion, making better choices and decisions, attaining happiness, peace and prosperity, this is what your life will mean to be. Change takes an instant. It is up to you, now, Coca. Do you want to change? Or do you want to continue your existence as it were? Do you want to interact with the world with a new way of thinking, feeling, perceiving and acting or do you want to go on reacting like you used to? Do you want to understand yourself more or do you still want to understand the world more? What is important in your life, Coca? What is it that you want? How do you want to create your future? Will you accept life as it comes? Will you love yourself? Answer me, Coca. Answer me. Answer me………."

And I awoke.

There was a warm tingly feeling in my whole body. I felt like I had been given a second life. The ocean looked beautiful. All the fish looked friendly. The anemone was warm and inviting. It looked like my new vision was working. The new way of seeing. But, the best thing was, I was comfortable in my own scales again. I was feeling good about myself. I felt loved, pampered and looked after. Like a new born baby. Hey! The questions were gone! Hurrah, joy was me! I was bouncing with joy when I heard the same soothing, caressing and loving voice say with a hint of humor no less, from within me, "Where true faith abides, there the questions disappear too! Go, Coca, go into the world and live the life you are supposed to live!"